W9-AAT-666

For older siblings
who took us under
your paw, and
younger siblings
who just want to
be part of it all!
— I.K.

NO SNOWBALL!

ISABELLA KUNG

Stretch

Buzzzz

Orchard Books
An Imprint of Scholastic Inc. • New York

Oh, hello.
You may have heard about me.
Yes, I am the one and only **Queen NoFuzzball.**
Hear my subjects chant my name.

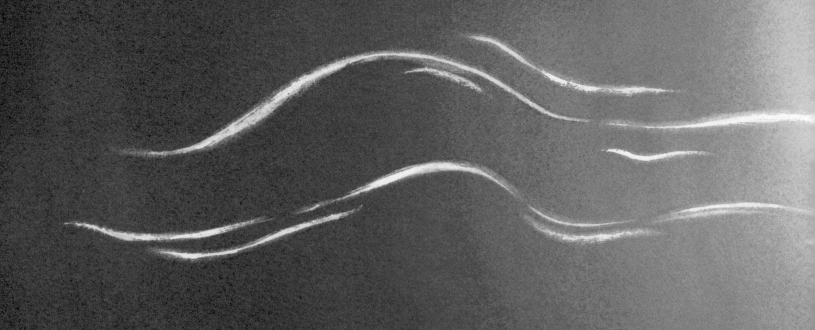

Look how
they worship
me constantly!

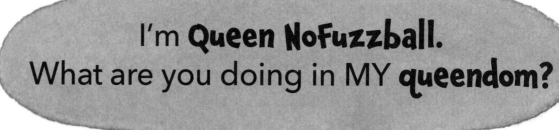

What an annoying
copycat!
She is the wor —

As I was saying, she is fearless to attack
something ten times her size!
Her landing is far from perfect, but
she could prove useful around
my queendom . . .

I can't believe
she failed every test!
This is not going to work.
How can she possibly
be a princess?

It is hopeless!

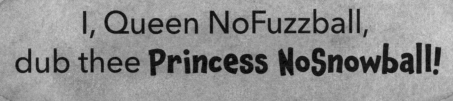

From now on, we shall rule this queendom **together.**